I once tried to fool the Tooth Fairy.

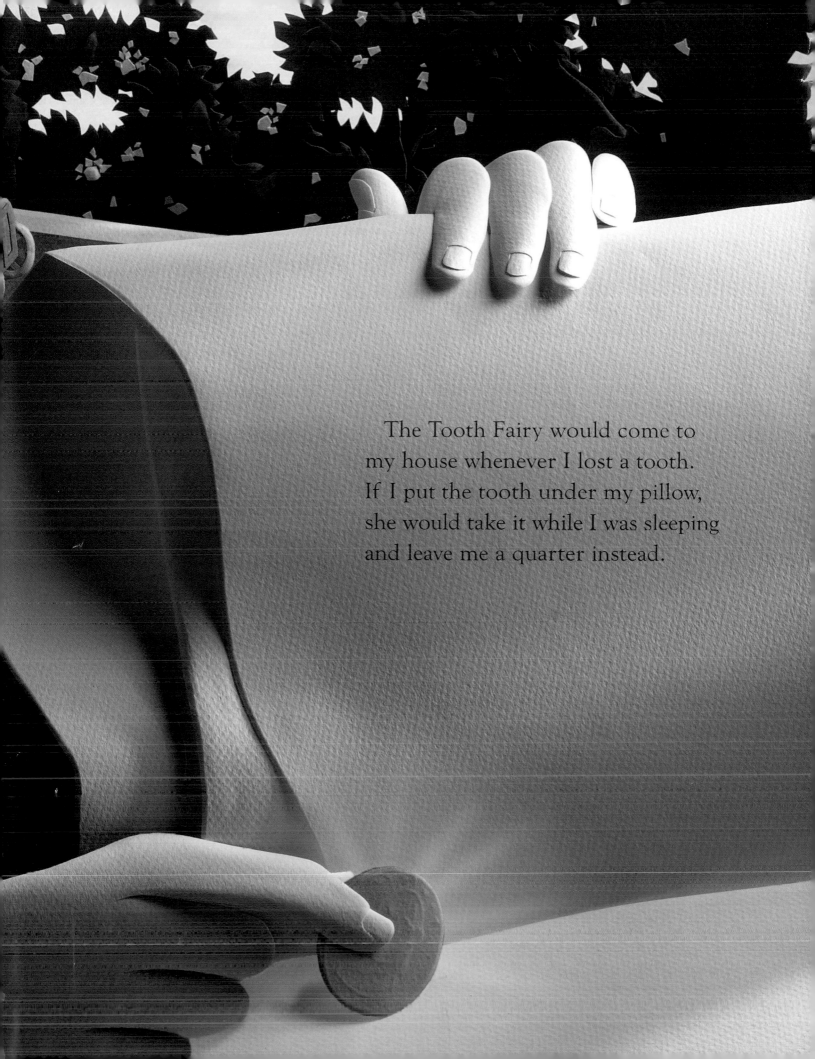

The Tooth Fairy would come to my house whenever I lost a tooth. If I put the tooth under my pillow, she would take it while I was sleeping and leave me a quarter instead.

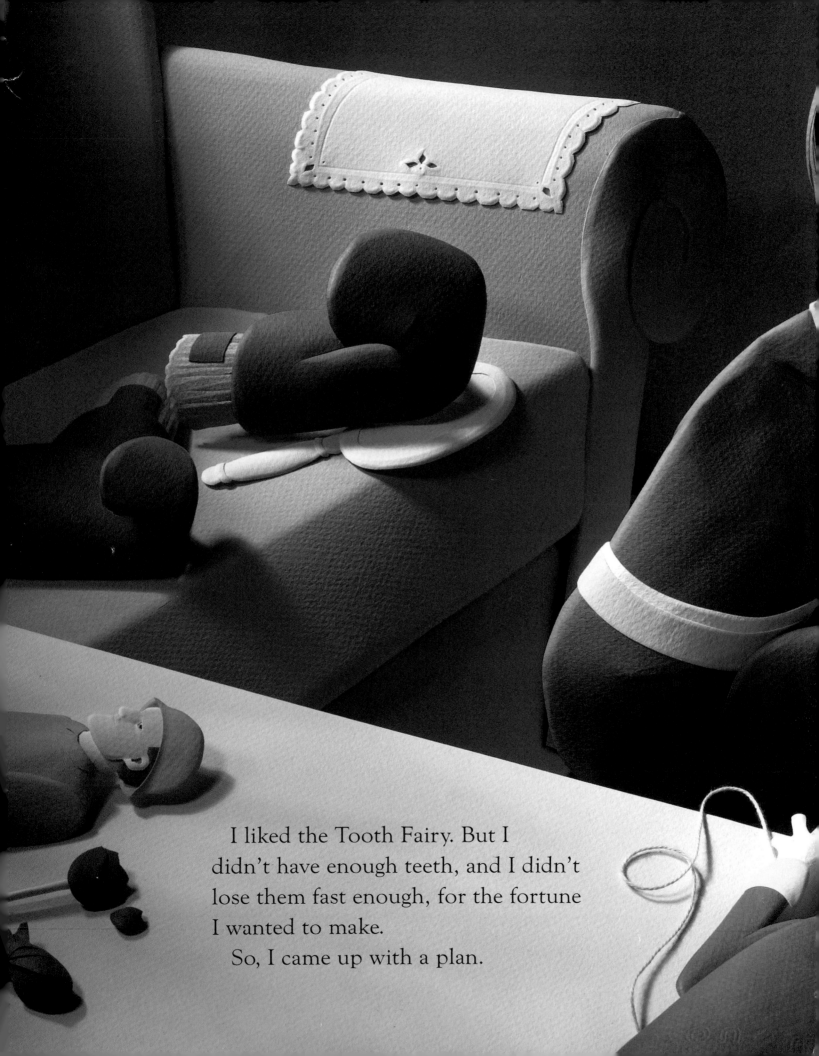

I liked the Tooth Fairy. But I
didn't have enough teeth, and I didn't
lose them fast enough, for the fortune
I wanted to make.

So, I came up with a plan.

I found some white paper and drew myself a tooth. Carefully, I cut the edges.

This was not hard work at all. So I made a second tooth, too. I would put these two "teeth" under my pillow and—if my plan worked—wake up rich the next day.

My mom wasn't so sure.

"The Tooth Fairy is very smart," she told me. "She might figure out that you are really playing a trick."

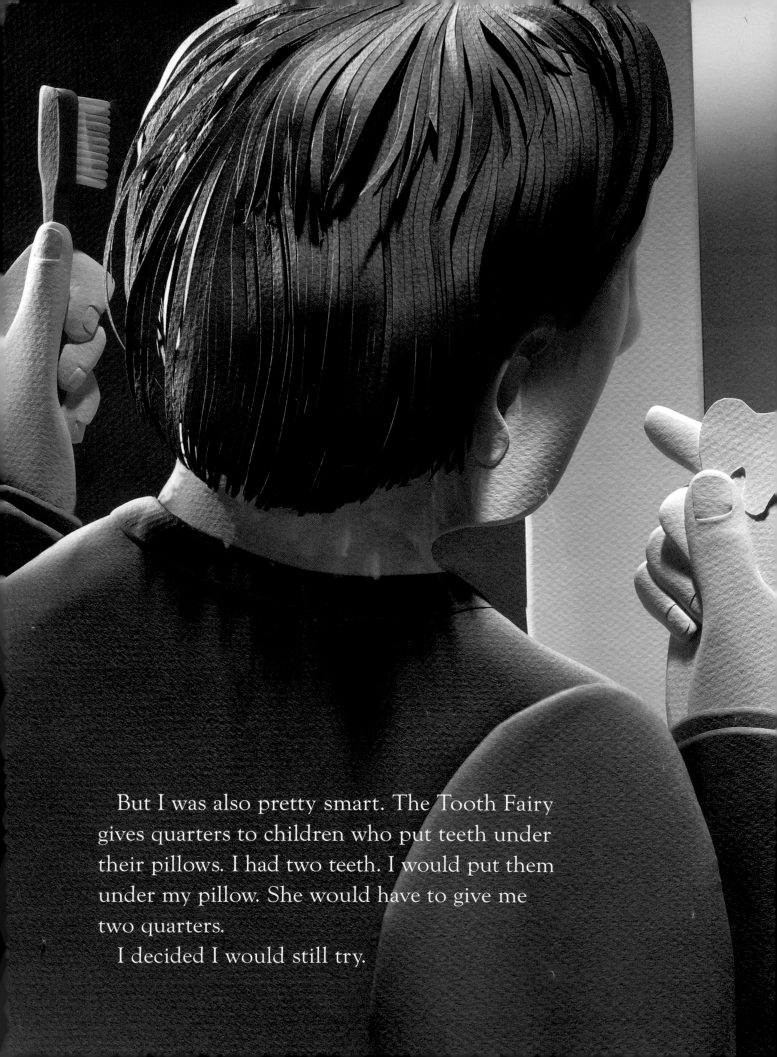

But I was also pretty smart. The Tooth Fairy gives quarters to children who put teeth under their pillows. I had two teeth. I would put them under my pillow. She would have to give me two quarters.

I decided I would still try.

That night, I slipped the two
paper teeth under my pillow.

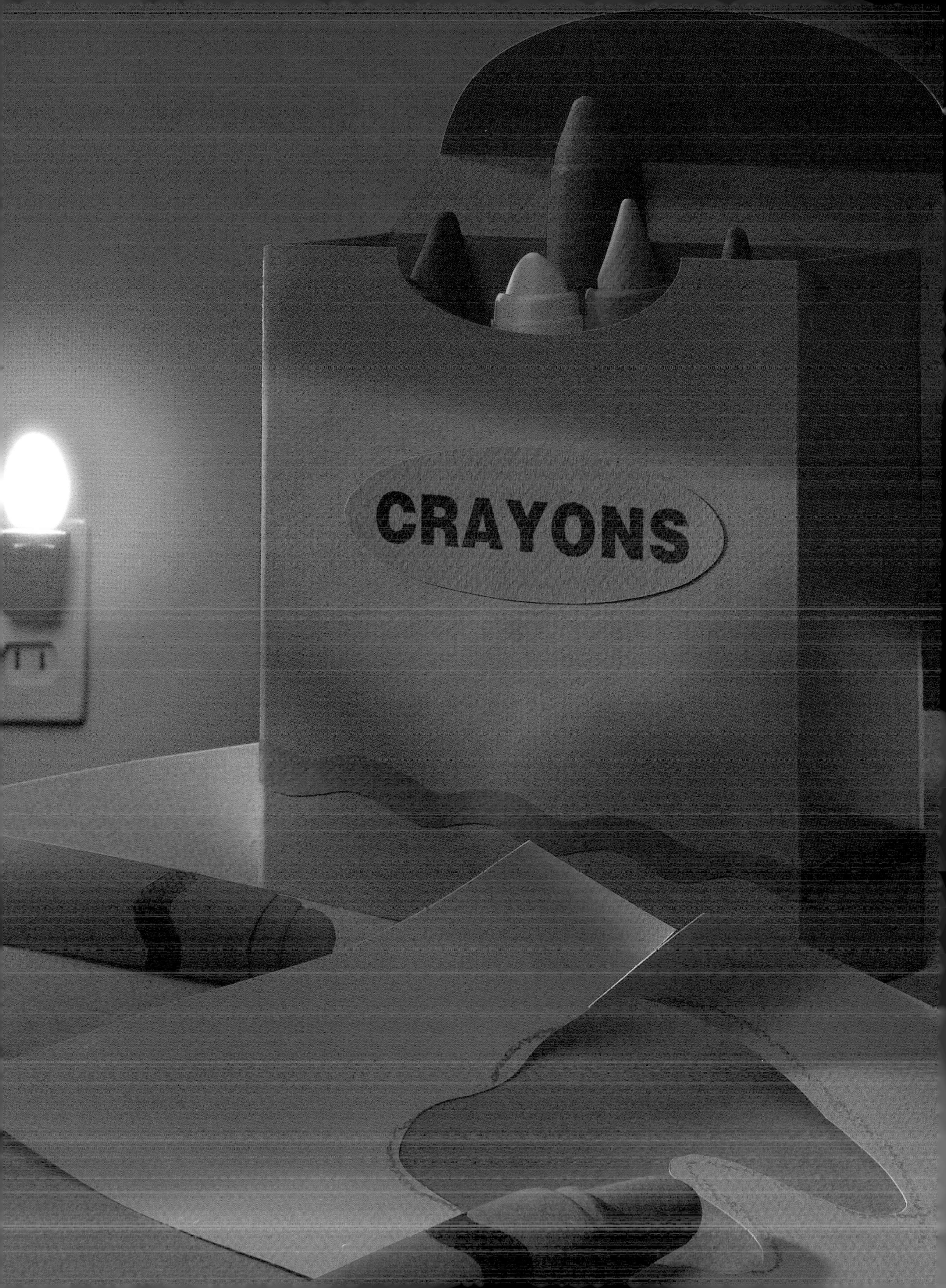
CRAYONS

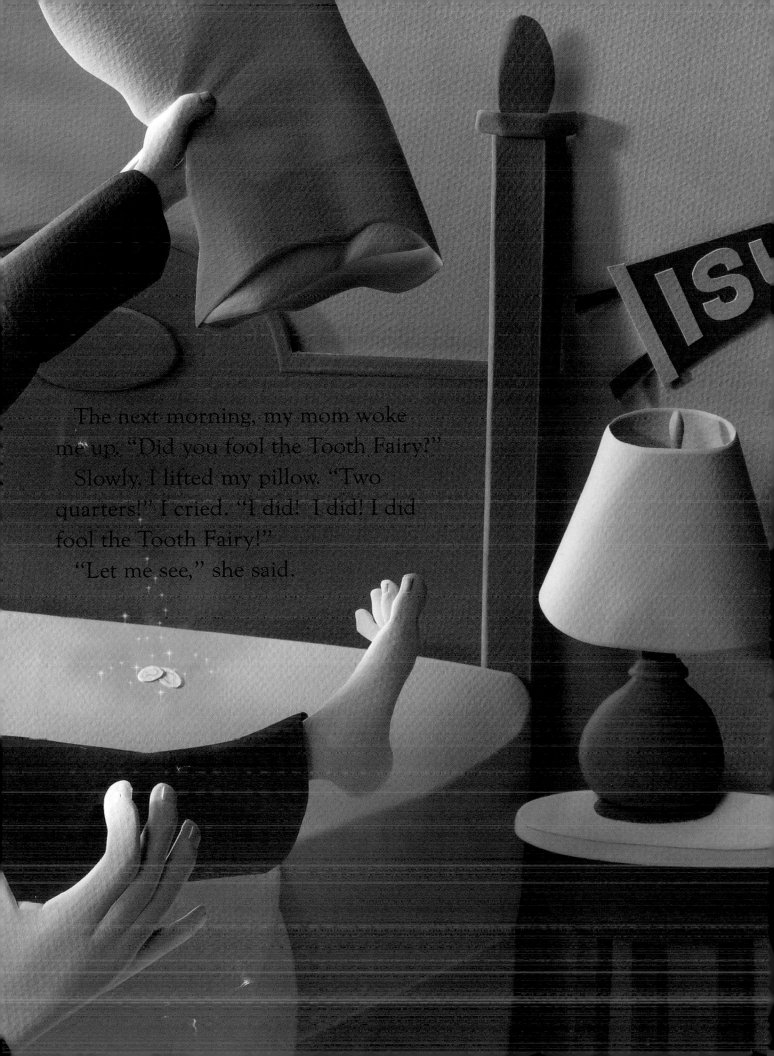

The next morning, my mom woke me up. "Did you fool the Tooth Fairy?"

Slowly, I lifted my pillow. "Two quarters!" I cried. "I did! I did! I did fool the Tooth Fairy!"

"Let me see," she said.

That's when I realized that something
was wrong. When I picked them up, I found out
why. They weren't quarters at all. The Tooth Fairy
had left me two circles of cut-out paper that she had
drawn to look like quarters. Just like my paper teeth.

"Somebody sure got fooled," said my mom. "But it
wasn't the Tooth Fairy."

There wasn't much I could do with two paper quarters but show them to my friends. And warn them.

"If you're planning to fool the Tooth Fairy," I'd say, "there's just one thing you need to know…

"She's smarter than you think."

A TRUE STORY

After nearly forty years, I realize my mom was right about the Tooth Fairy.

But what most amazes me now is not how the Tooth Fairy can outwit those who would deceive her. Instead, I marvel that no matter how small the chance of success, children never give up trying.

I don't really think that I was the first to try to fool the Tooth Fairy. I know for sure, however, that I won't be the last.

Martin Nelson Burton
La Cañada Flintridge, California

For Mom
—MNB

For the three toothless grins that bless the Hansen home.
They are my inspiration and joy.
—CH

Photographer Dean Tanner stages Clint Hansen's artwork.

The illustrations were created in paper sculpture. In this medium, construction paper is cut, shaped, and then glued together in multiple layers to form three-dimensional figures. Each piece is then positioned on an illuminated studio set, and the finished scene is photographed.

Photography by Dean Tanner of Primary Image, Des Moines, Iowa.

London Town Press P.O. Box 585   Montrose, California 91021.
www.LondonTownPress.com

Distributed by Publishers Group West
Printed in Singapore

Book design by Christy Hale.
10 9 8 7 6 5 4 3 2 1

Publisher's Cataloging-in-Publication Data
Burton, Martin Nelson.
Fooling the Tooth Fairy / by Martin Nelson Burton ; illustrated by Clint Hansen.
p. cm.
Summary: When a boy tries to fool the Tooth Fairy by leaving paper teeth,
she turns out to be smarter than he thinks.
Audience: Ages 4-8.
LCCN 2004094372
ISBN 0-9666490-2-8
1. Tooth Fairy (Legendary character)—Juvenile fiction.
[1. Tooth Fairy—Fiction. 2. Deception—Fiction.] I. Hansen, Clint. II. Title
PZ7.B9535Foo 2005   [E]